MW00934841

FIRST STAR

A BEAR AND MOLE STORY

WILL HILLENBRAND

HOLIDAY HOUSE · NEW YORK

Copyright © 2018 by Will Hillenbrand
All Rights Reserved
HOLIDAY HOUSE is registered in the U.S. Patent and Trademark Office.
Printed and bound in June 2018 at Toppan Leefung, DongGuan City, China.
The artwork was created with direct impression media and pencil.
www.holidayhouse.com
First Edition
3 5 7 9 10 8 6 4

Library of Congress Cataloging-in-Publication Data

Names: Hillenbrand, Will, author, illustrator.
Title: First star : a Bear and Mole story / Will Hillenbrand.
Description: First edition. | New York : Holiday House, [2018]
Summary: While camping, Bear tells Mole the story of how the First Bears created
   the moon and the stars.
Identifiers: LCCN 2016050982 | ISBN 9780823437603 (hardcover)
Subjects: | CYAC: Stars—Fiction. | Camping—Fiction. | Bears—Fiction. |
   Moles (Animals)—Fiction.
Classification: LCC PZ7.H55773 Fi 2018 | DDC [E]—dc23 LC record available
   at https://lccn.loc.gov/2016050982

To Dean Regas and my friends at the Cincinnati
Observatory who keep me looking UP!
With a special thanks to the good people
involved with PA ONE Book. You encouraged
me to make our LITTLE STARS shine!

Mole gazed up.

"May we sleep under the sky tonight?" asked Mole.

"I want to see the stars turn on."

"We can hike
to Camp Tiptop," said Bear.

"Will we get lost in the dark up there?" wondered Mole.

"No," said Bear.
"We'll be together."

"Okay, let's go," said Mole.

Bear rolled.

Mole stuffed.

They put on their packs.

Mole climbed
UP, UP, UP.

Bear picked,
YUM,
YUM,
YUM.

Together they clambered.

Then they made camp.

"Will it be getting dark soon?"
asked Mole.

"Not for a while,"
replied Bear.

"I don't want to get lost
in the dark," whimpered
Mole. "Let's go
back home!"

"I'll tell you the story of First Star," said Bear.

"It will tell you how to find your way."

Long ago, First Father Bear,
First Mother Bear, and First
Baby Bear lived here.

They played,
they bathed, and they
ate lots of berries,
just like all bears.

But they worried.

The night was always
VERY,
VERY DARK.

They could not see.

So, First Little Bear helped his mother
dig up white clay.

They shaped it into a ball. The ball was Moon.
Moon shone brightly.

"Look, Bear, I
see a funny face
on Moon!"
called Mole.

Then, First Little Bear scattered white stones into the darkness.

They became the stars.

"Bear, look! I see the white stones, I mean the stars." Mole chuckled.

After that, First Father Bear
reached up high.

He pushed
**HARD,
HARD,
HARD**
on one star.

"This star **WILL NOT** move!" he said.

"It will always point North.
We will never be lost in the dark."

He named it FIRST STAR.

First Father Bear then made a star
picture of First Little Bear.

First Star became his tail.

"I see his tail." Mole giggled.

"Dark is not so dark if you know where you are," Bear said, smiling.

"What is **THAT?**" marveled Mole.
"It's flying across the sky."

"It's your LUCKY star,"
said Bear. "Now, make a wish!"